EYE IN THE SKY

Adapted by Apple Jordan from the script
"Eye of the Beholder" by Jack Monaco, John Loy, and Ford Riley
for the series developed for television by Ford Riley

Illustrated by Francesco Legramandi and Gabriella Matta

A GOLDEN BOOK • NEW YORK

Copyright © 2016 Disney Enterprises, Inc. All rights reserved. Published in the United
States by Golden Books, an imprint of Random House Children's Books, a division of
Penguin Random House LLC, 1745 Broadway, New York, NY 10019, and in Canada
by Penguin Random House Canada Limited, Toronto, in conjunction with Disney
Enterprises, Inc. Golden Books, A Golden Book, A Little Golden Book,
the G colophon, and the distinctive gold spine are registered trademarks
of Penguin Random House LLC.
randomhousekids.com
ISBN 978-0-7364-3500-0 (trade) — ISBN 978-0-7364-3501-7 (ebook)
Printed in the United States of America
10 9 8 7 6 5 4 3 2 1

It is another busy day in the Pride Lands. Janja and his hyena crew are up to no good—again. They are chasing a herd of gnu, and the members of the Lion Guard are determined to stop them.

"Look out!" Ono the egret shouts. He warns Kion and Fuli of a scared gnu heading straight for them. The fierce lion and fast cheetah jump out of the way just in time.

"Good eyes!" Kion calls up to Ono. "Now be on the lookout for Janja and his gang."

Ono spots two of the hyenas, Chungu and Cheezi, and warns his friends below.

"Let's get 'em, Beshte!" Bunga says. The honey badger holds on tight to the hippo as they chase the hyenas off into the dust.

"That takes care of those two!" Ono says.

Hidden in the dust caused by the gnu stampede, Janja sneaks up on Kion. "Gotcha now, lion cub," he says with an evil grin.

Ono spots the sly hyena. "Kion!" he calls down. "Look out behind you!"

Kion turns to see Janja leaping toward him. But the lion has a plan—thanks to Ono, his eye in the sky. Ono tells Kion that a gnu is charging straight at them. Kion pushes the hyena into the gnu's path. The gnu crashes into Janja, sending him flying.

As the hyenas run off, Ono is hit in the eye with a flying rock.

"Ow!" Ono cries. He covers his eye with his wing.

The Lion Guard quickly carry Ono back to the Lion Guard Lair to see Rafiki, the Royal Advisor.

"He'll know what to do," says Kion.

Rafiki the wise baboon puts a mixture of smashed bananas and mud on Ono's eye. Then he covers it with a patch.

"Wear this eye patch for three days," Rafiki tells the egret. "And no flying!"

Rafiki is not just an advisor. He is also an artist. He shows the Guard his new painting. It is a large picture of Kion, with smaller pictures of Fuli, Beshte, Bunga, and Ono around him. But it is missing something.

"My painting does not quite have the spirit of your Lion Guard," Rafiki says.

Meanwhile, in the Outlands, the hyenas are listening in on some vultures. The vultures always know what is going on in the Pride Lands.

"It seems Ono is no longer able to see out of one eye," the vulture Mwoga reports.

Janja flashes an evil grin. Without Ono as the Guard's lookout, the hyenas will be able to trap the Lion Guard—and get them out of the way once and for all!

"Then we'll be able to feast in the Pride Lands as much as we want!" Janja says to Cheezi and Chungu.

Back in the Lion Guard Lair, Beshte reports that the hyenas are in the Pride Lands again, near a grazing herd of zebras.

Kion orders the Lion Guard into action. "Till the Pride Land's end, Lion Guard defend!" he shouts.

Everyone rushes to the rescue. Everyone except Ono, who is left behind.

"*MOST* of the Lion Guard defend," Ono sighs.

Meanwhile, at the top of the canyon, the hyenas are busy building a giant wall of boulders and rocks. The zebras are grazing peacefully in the plains below.

"Why are we doing this, Janja?" Cheezi asks. "We can't eat rocks."

"It's part of my plan to trap the Lion Guard," say Janja. "The zebras are just the bait."

When Kion and the gang arrive at the base of the canyon, the hyenas push the boulders and rocks. They crash down in front of the Lion Guard.

The Guard turns to run, but the hyenas push more boulders and block their escape. There is no way out!

"You fell right into my trap," Janja laughs from above. "Or my trap fell right onto *YOU*! Now let's get those zebras!" he says to Cheezi and Chungu.

"Hurry, Kion!" says Bunga. "Use your roar to blast us out of here!"

But Kion is worried about the zebras on the other side of the wall. "The rocks could fly out and hurt them," he says.

Beshte tries to move a large rock, but the wall starts to fall. It's too dangerous.

Just then, Ono flies overhead. "Eye or no eye, my place is with the Guard!" he says. Everyone is excited to see him.

"I need to blast these rocks," Kion yells up to Ono. "But first you have to warn the zebras to get away from the canyon."

"You got it!" says Ono, and he flies away. He is happy to be needed again.

Ono tries to get the zebras' attention, but they are too busy eating their lunch.

The egret gets an idea. He flies off in a hurry, pumping his wings to go higher and higher.

Ono turns and dives toward the ground like a missile. He buzzes right past the zebras, sending them into a panicked run.

"I knew I could get you to move!" says Ono triumphantly. He rushes back to tell Kion that all is clear.

Kion lets out a giant **ROAR**! The power of his roar smashes the rock wall and causes the hyenas to fall off the top of the canyon.

"You haven't seen the last of me!" Janja yells to the Lion Guard as he runs off with Chungu and Cheezi.

"Good job, Ono," says Kion. "We couldn't have done it without you!"

Back at the Lion Guard Lair, Rafiki removes Ono's bandage. "I can see great!" Ono says.

Rafiki also reveals his finished painting. Now all the Guard members are the same size. "I figured out what was missing," Rafiki tells them. "Kion does not just lead you—you are all friends. This Lion Guard is best when you're all together."

"It's perfect," says Kion. And everyone agrees—especially Ono.